Dedicated to all those who open their hearts
and homes to furry friends—E.D.T.

Lots of Cats
Copyright © 2018 by E. Dee Taylor
All rights reserved. Manufactured in China.
No part of this book may be used or reproduced in any manner whatsoever without
written permission except in the case of brief quotations embodied in critical articles
and reviews. For information address HarperCollins Children's Books, a division of
HarperCollins Publishers, 195 Broadway, New York, NY 10007.
www.harpercollinschildrens.com

ISBN 978-0-06-267569-9

The artist used Prismacolor colored pencils on Arches hot press paper, with a smidge
of gouache and watercolors, to create the illustrations for this book.
Typography by Erica De Chavez
18 19 20 21 22 SCP 10 9 8 7 6 5 4 3 2 1 ❖ First Edition

LOTS of CATS

by E. Dee Taylor

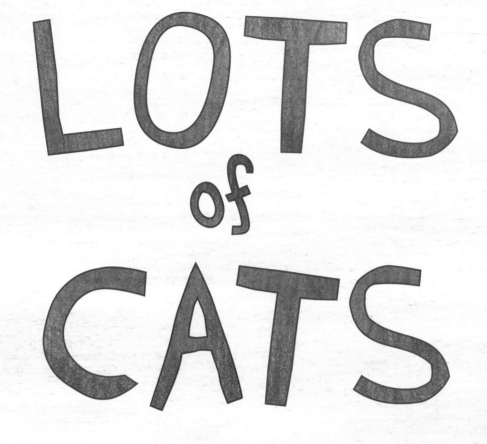

HARPER

An Imprint of HarperCollinsPublishers

Margaret was an independent little witch.

Many things kept her busy,

but sometimes

she longed for someone to play with.

So one day Margaret experimented with
a spell, hoping to conjure up a friend.

Purrigee furrigee . . .
zurrigee . . . zate . . .
These are the words
to make a playmate.

She added an extra amount of
each potion to ensure it would work.

It was maybe a bit too much.

Margaret didn't
see a new friend—but
she could hear noises
coming from outside.

When she opened the door,
Margaret saw a bunch of CATS!

They immediately made themselves at home.

HOME
SWEET
HOME

Hello, cat!

Margaret was curious about what sorts of activities the cats would enjoy.

A broomstick-extension spell made room for all of them to take a midnight ride.

Having lots of cats

was a lot of fun.

But . . .

it was also a lot of food,

a lot of poop,

a lot of hair,

and a lot of mess.

Margaret couldn't find magic words
that would make cats follow directions.
However, she did think of something
that could make them disappear.

It was nice to be alone again.

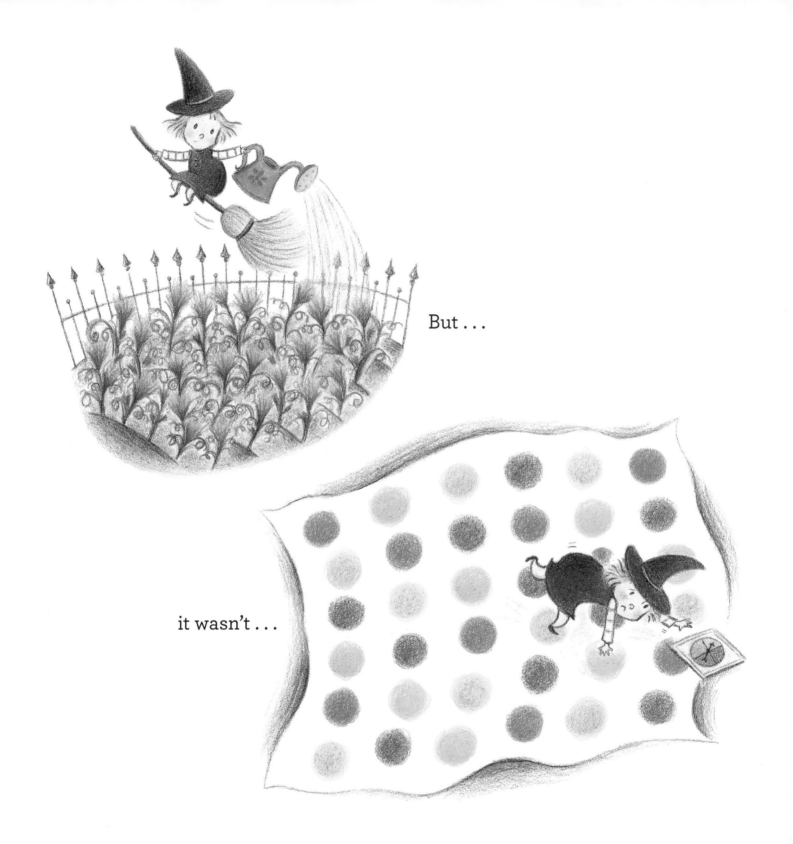

But . . .

it wasn't . . .

. . . quite as nice as before.

Margaret tried a spell to bring the cats back.

Kooky-ooky-mooky-mon,
I don't know where the cats have gone!
Pooky-snooky-hooky-hay,
return them all without delay!

Poof!

Poof!

poof!

I said CATS!

Then she made a potion to show her where the cats were. It didn't work, either.

So Margaret set out to search for the cats. She called to them, hoping to hear their meows.

CATS?

HOO! HOO!

She looked high,

and she looked low.

CATS?

S-SSSSS!

Margaret didn't find the cats. They were gone.

That night Margaret dreamed of a magic
spell that brought her furry friends back home.

And when she woke up, there they were!